7/5

P
FOR

WAR
AND PEAS

MICHAEL FOREMAN

HAMISH HAMILTON

King Lion looked around his country and was sad.
For a long time there had been no rain, and the ground
was hard and dry. Nothing could grow, and there was
nothing left to eat.
The birds had flown off to collect seeds, while the bigger
animals tried in vain to break up the ground for planting.

In a nearby country there was plenty of food.
King Lion told his people he would have to ask their rich
neighbour for help.

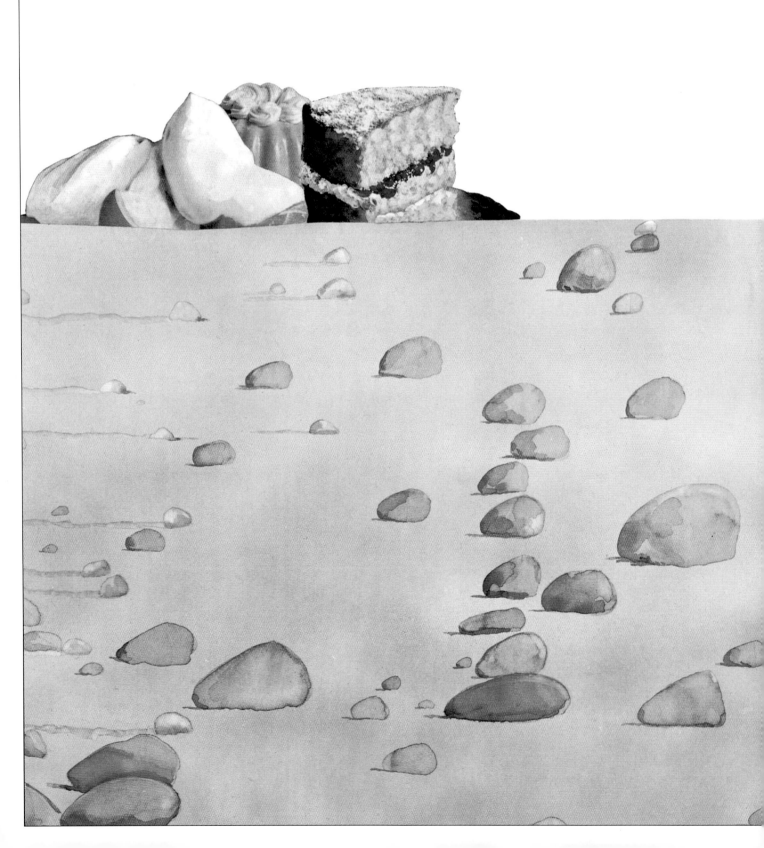

He set off, taking with him the Minister for Food, who worked in a grocery shop. It was a long journey, and the Lion told the young Grocer stories about the days when their country stretched across the world, and the animals roamed through forests and across broad grasslands. At last they saw in the distance the hills of the neighbouring kingdom.

As they approached the city they were much impressed
by the richness of everything.
"Surely they have more than they need," said the Grocer
hopefully.

Suddenly the Lion and the Grocer
were seized by guards and taken
to the main square.

And there, with all his portly courtiers, was the fattest king they had ever seen. "What do you animals mean by trespassing in my country?" roared the Fat King.

"Sire, I am a king like yourself –" began the Lion.

"Never!" yelled the Fat King. "You are too thin to be a king. Lock them up!"

"We only came to ask for any extra food you might have,"
said the Grocer nervously. "Our people are starving."
"Beggars, are you?" shouted the Fat King. "Why should we
go to the bother of sending you food? It is too much trouble."
"We'd be glad to come and get it," said the Lion.
"ROBBERS!" bellowed the Fat King. "Arrest them! Burrrp!
Now they've given me indigestion."

The Lion and the Grocer struggled free. They leaped on their bicycles and pedalled away as fast as they could go. Behind them was the entire fat army.

But the soldiers were *too* fat. The men in the tanks were
so big that the drivers had no elbow room and couldn't
steer properly. Tyres on the trucks burst under the weight,
and the trucks trundled along on the wheel rims.
And the cavalry was useless!

The fat army ploughed across the country after the Lion and the Grocer, followed by the Fat King and trucks full of supplies for the fat soldiers.

Their progress was so slow that the Lion and the Grocer had plenty of time to sound the alarm. When the Fat King, his army and his supply trucks arrived, the animals were ready for them.

Before the fat soldiers could stop them, the animals had jumped on the supply trucks. The fat army was bombarded on all sides.

Then the birds came back with hundreds of seeds.

It began to rain.

The earth turned to mud, and the soldiers stuck fast.
"Enough! We've had enough!" cried the Fat King. "Help!"
"Help yourself," said the Lion, as a strawberry cream pie sailed
through the air towards the Fat King. "You went to great trouble
to supply your army, but you would not bother to feed a hungry
country."

Then the Lion looked at the defeated Fat King and smiled. "But you *have* helped us, after all," he said. "Just look at those fields. Your army trucks have dug up our land and now the seeds will grow. There will be plenty for everyone!"

"Burrrp!" said the Fat King.
"Peace," said the Lion.
"No, no, no," groaned the Fat King,
"don't mention peas, ever."
"Peace," repeated the Lion.
"Never heard of it," said the Fat King.
"What's the recipe?"

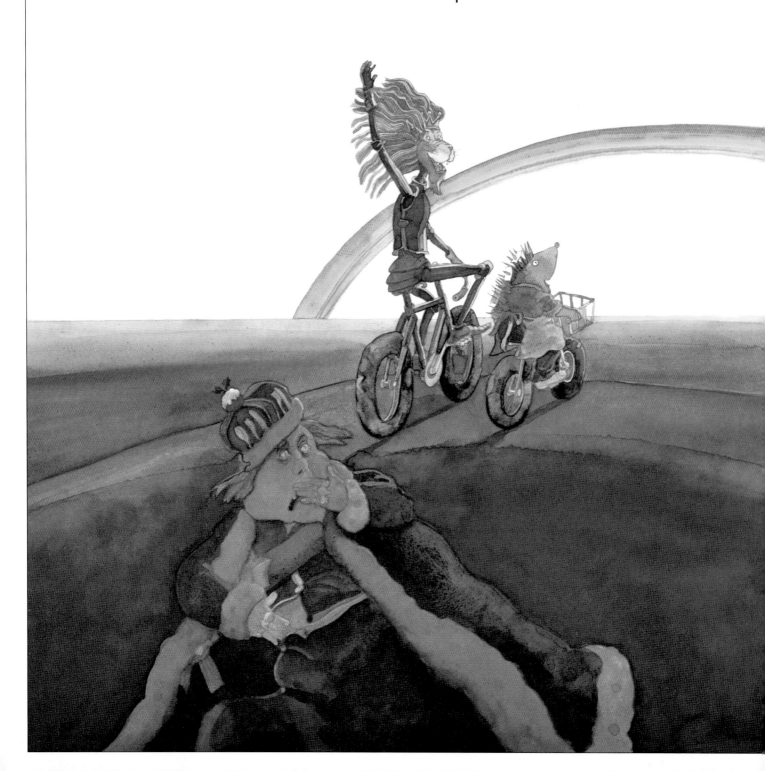

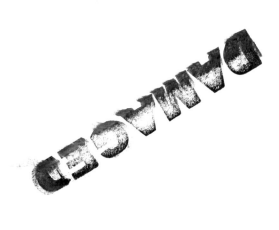

DAMAGED